The Spies

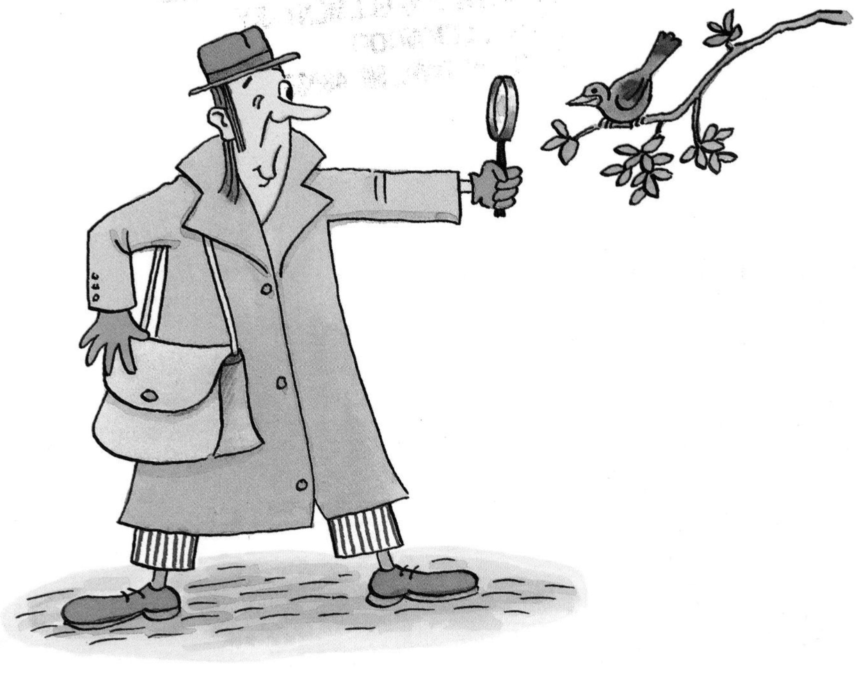

Illustrated by Trevor Pye

Rigby

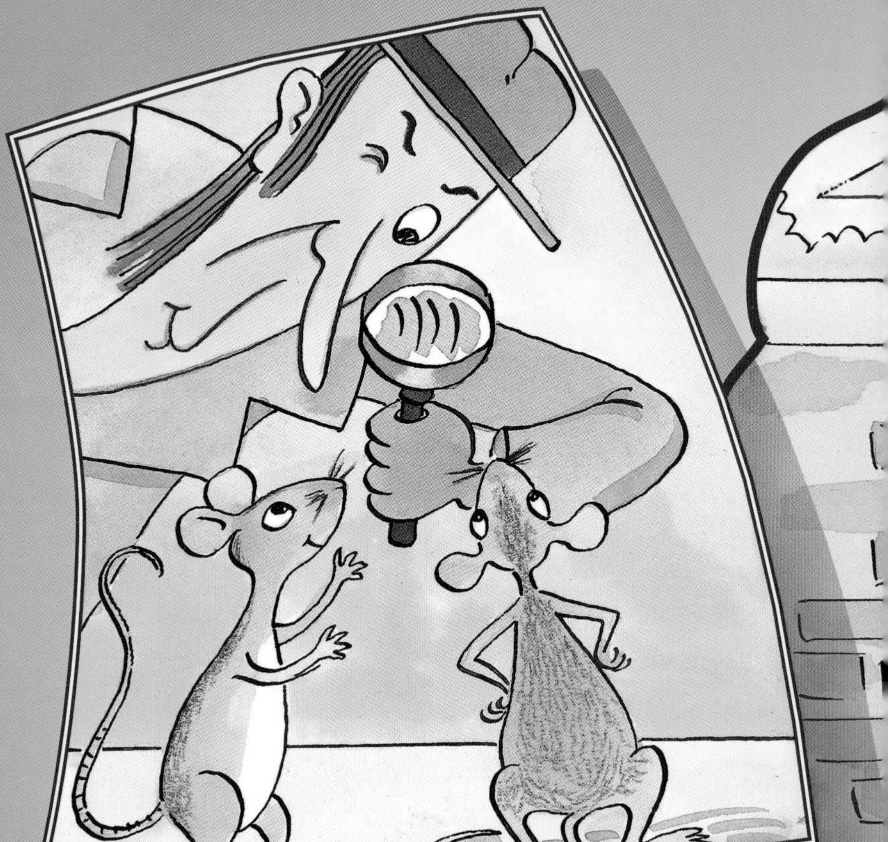

Here are the mice.

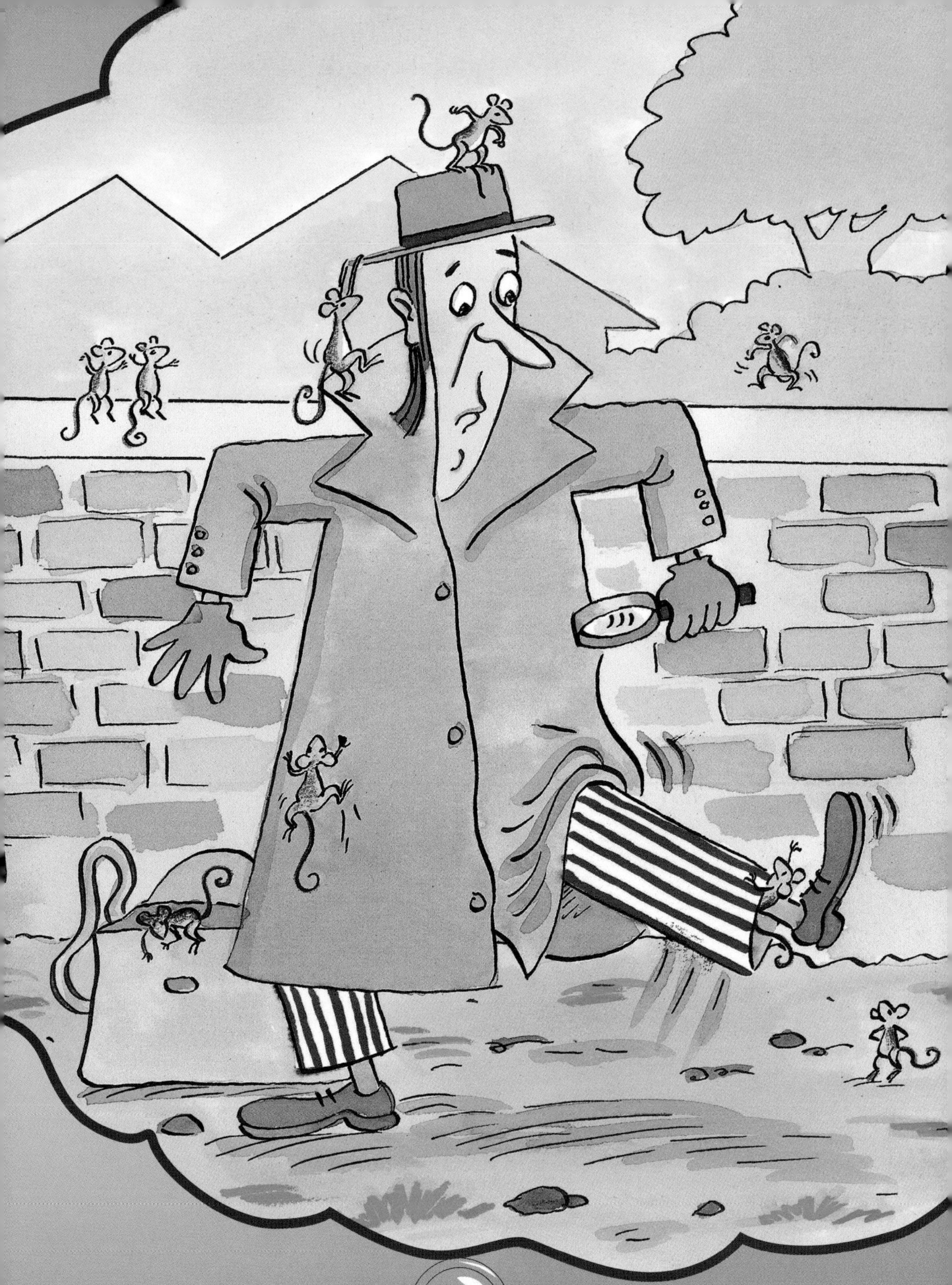

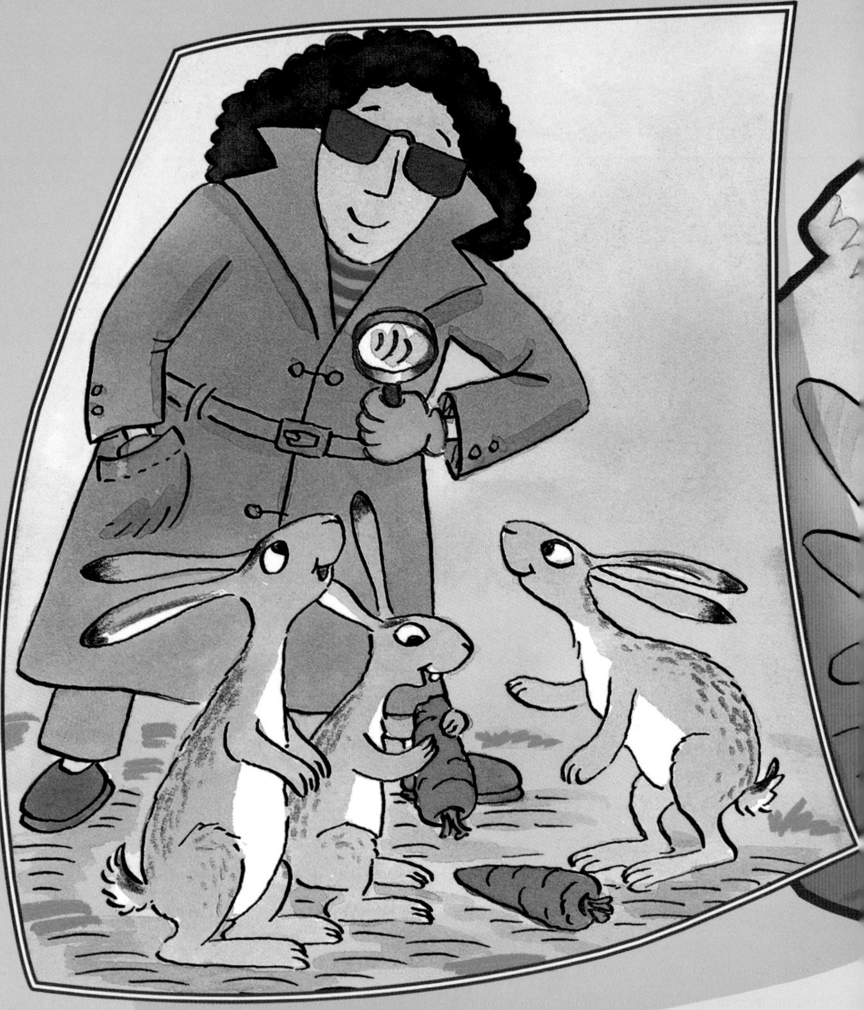

Here are the rabbits.

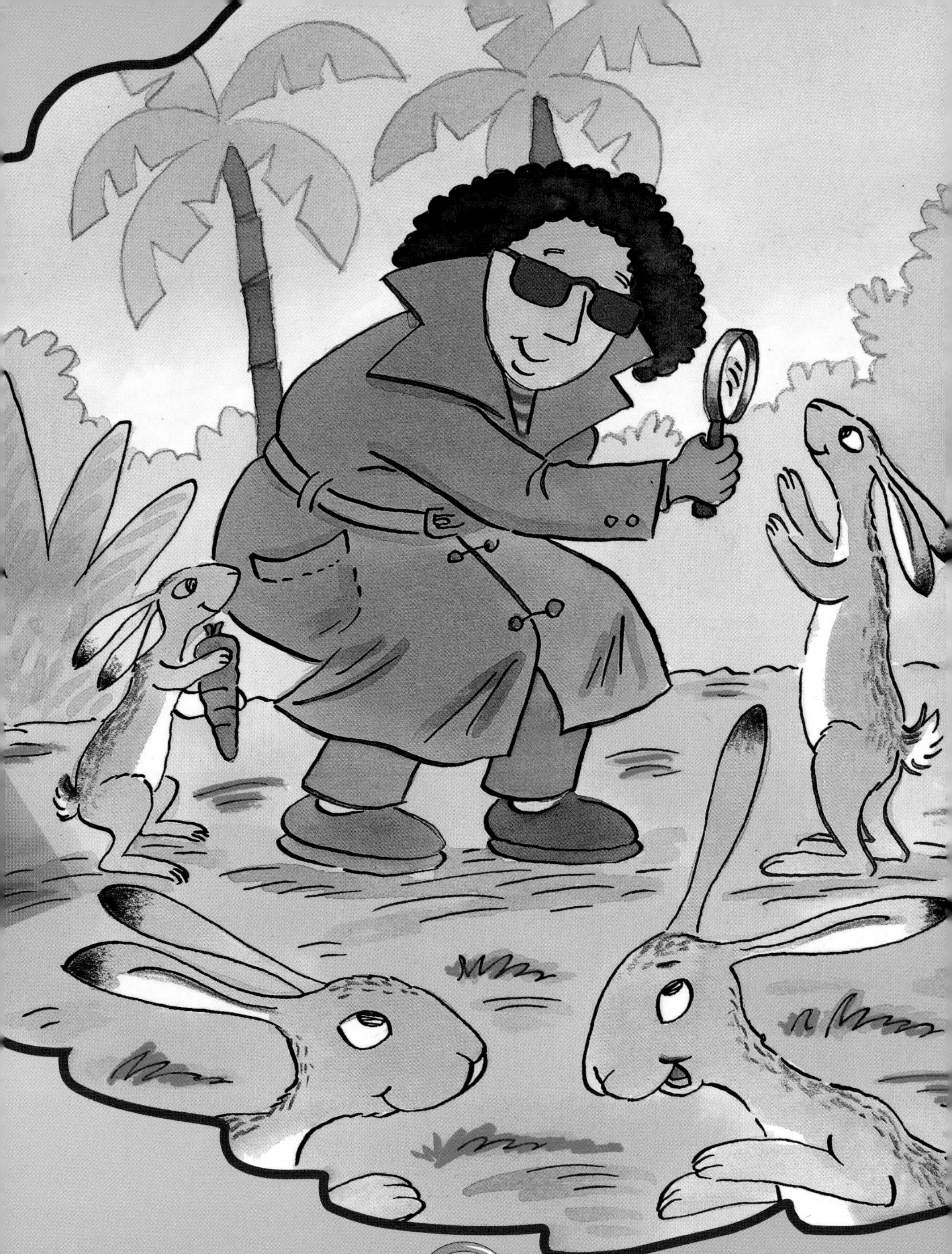

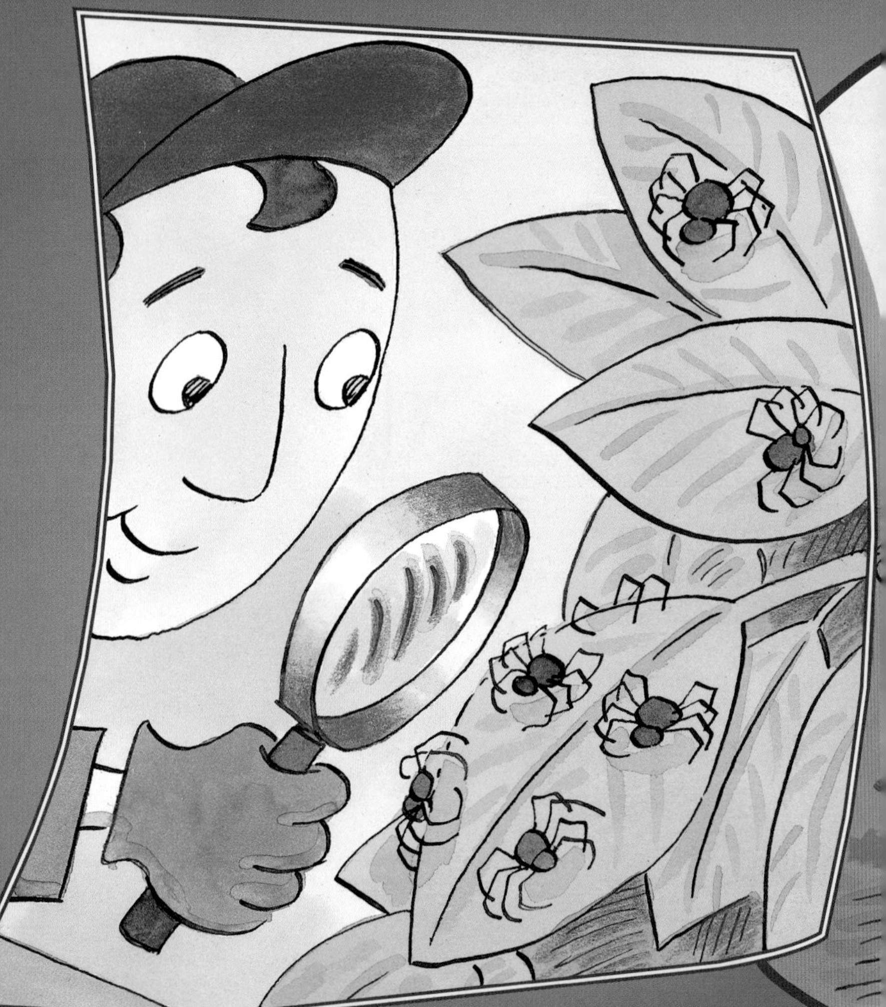

Here are the spiders.

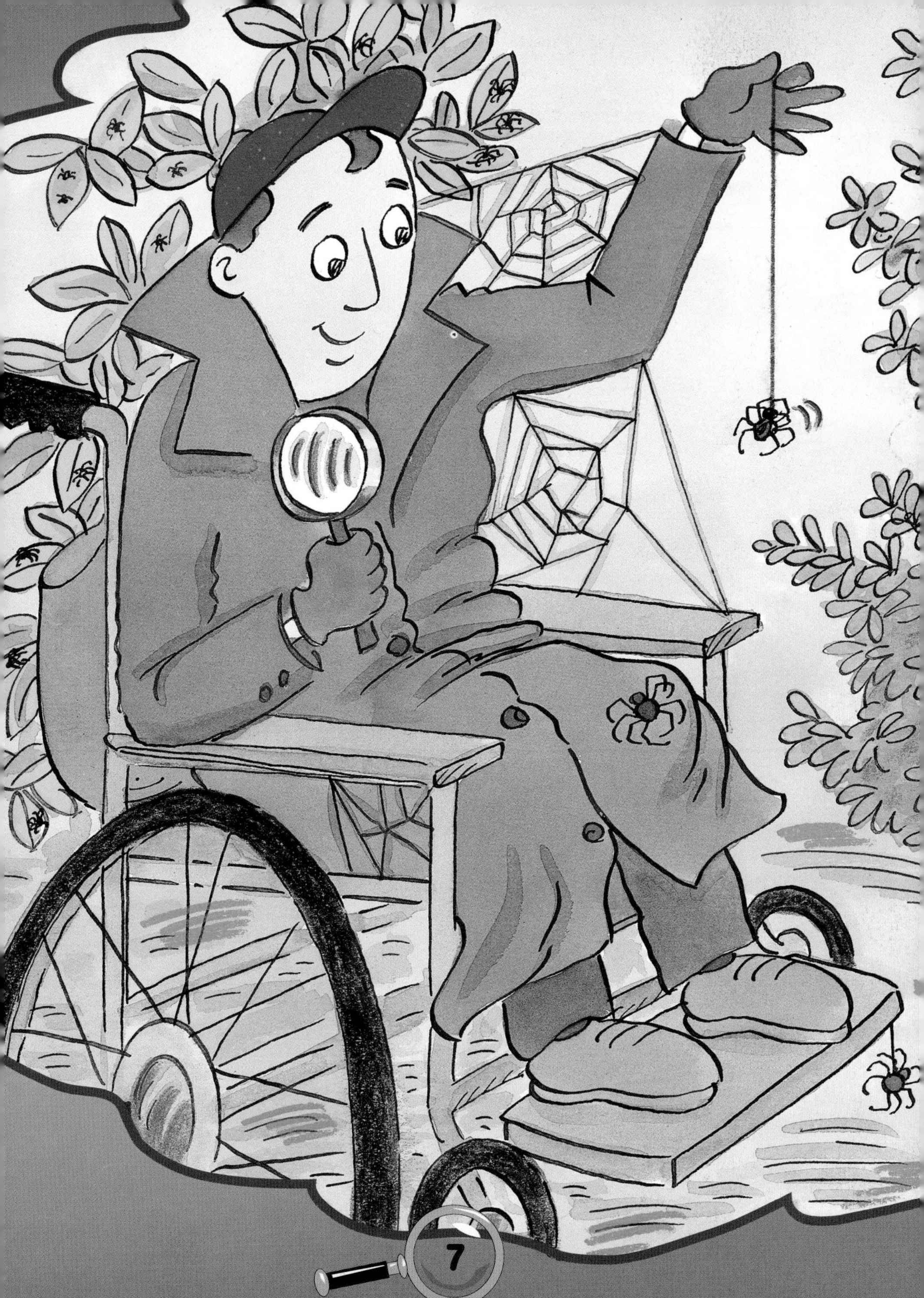

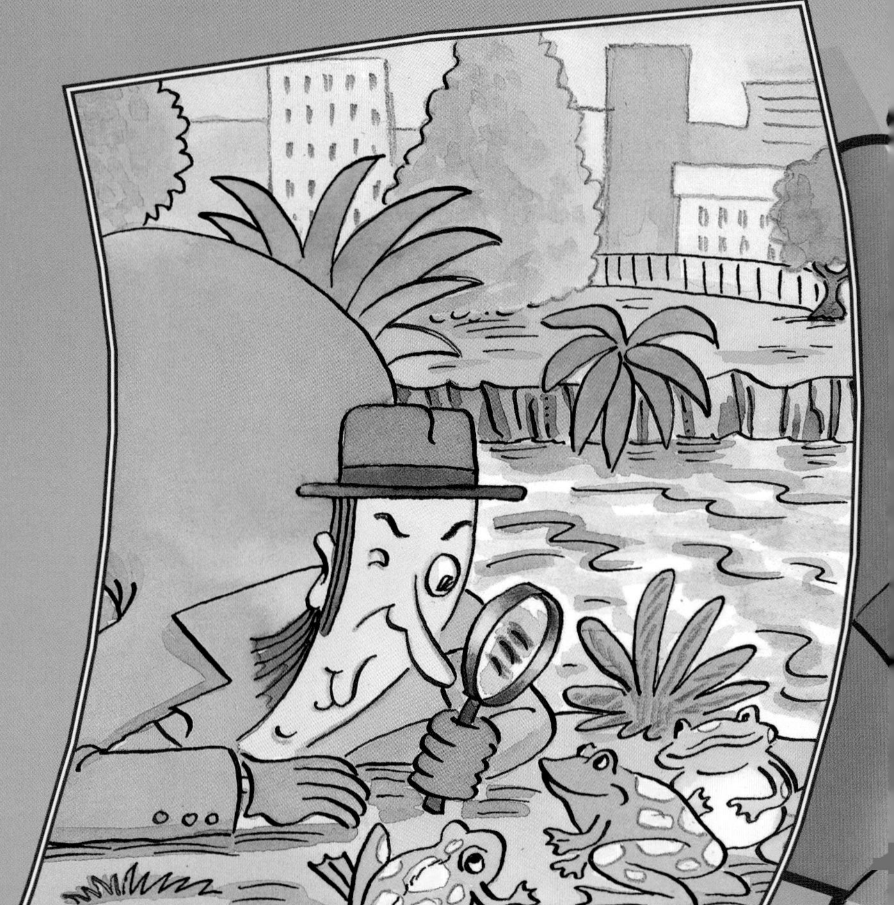

Here are the frogs.

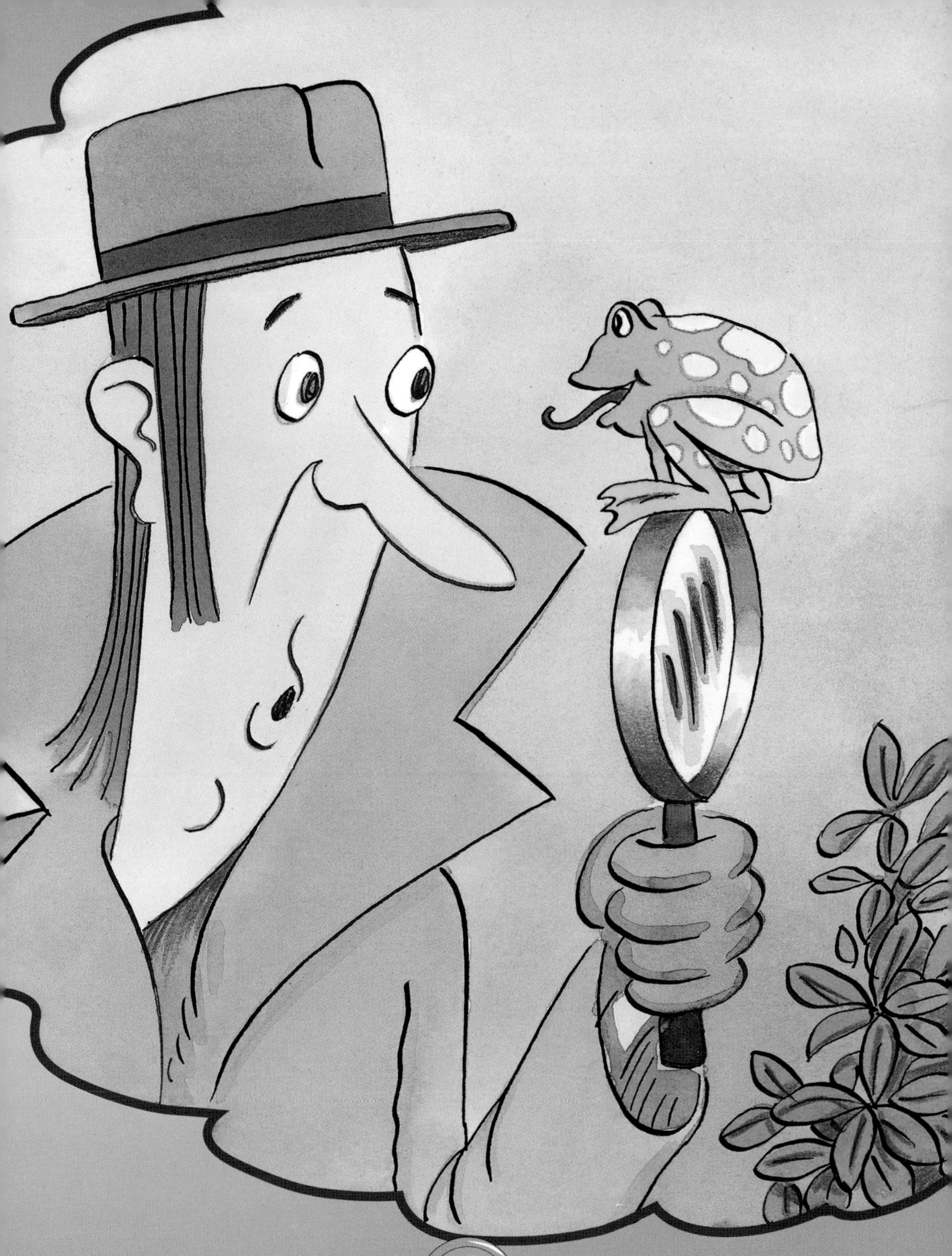

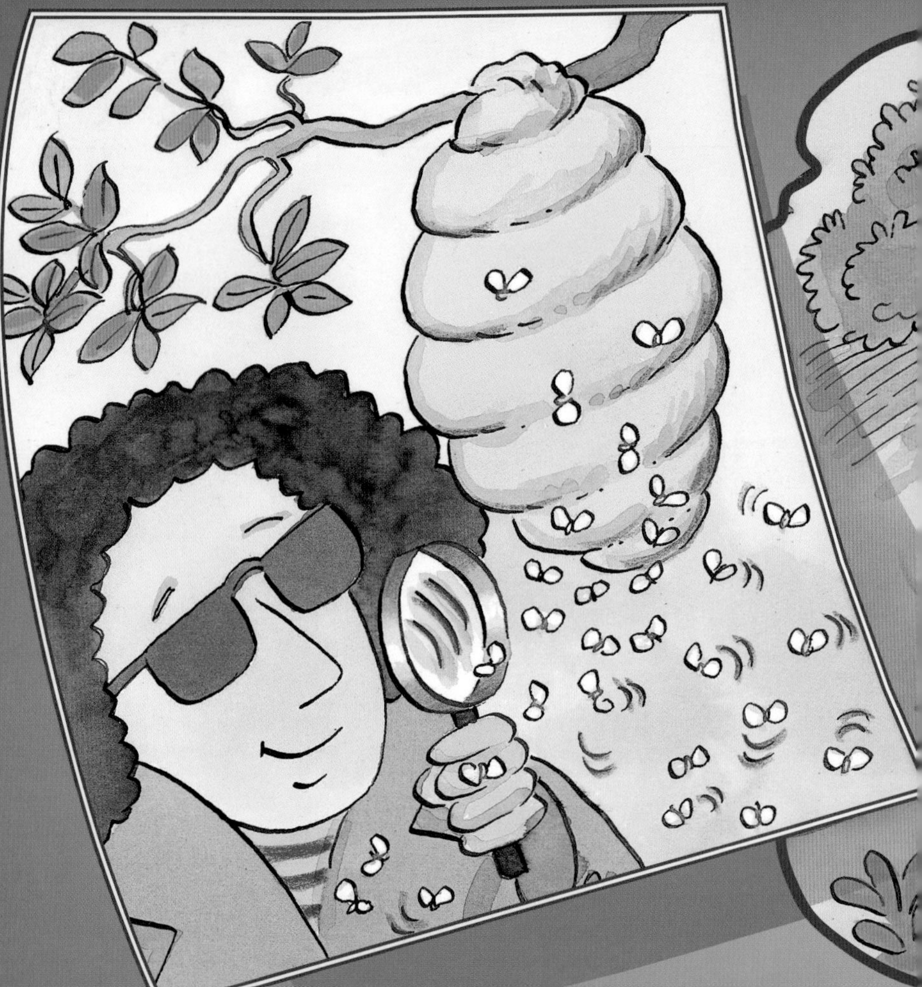

Here are the bees.

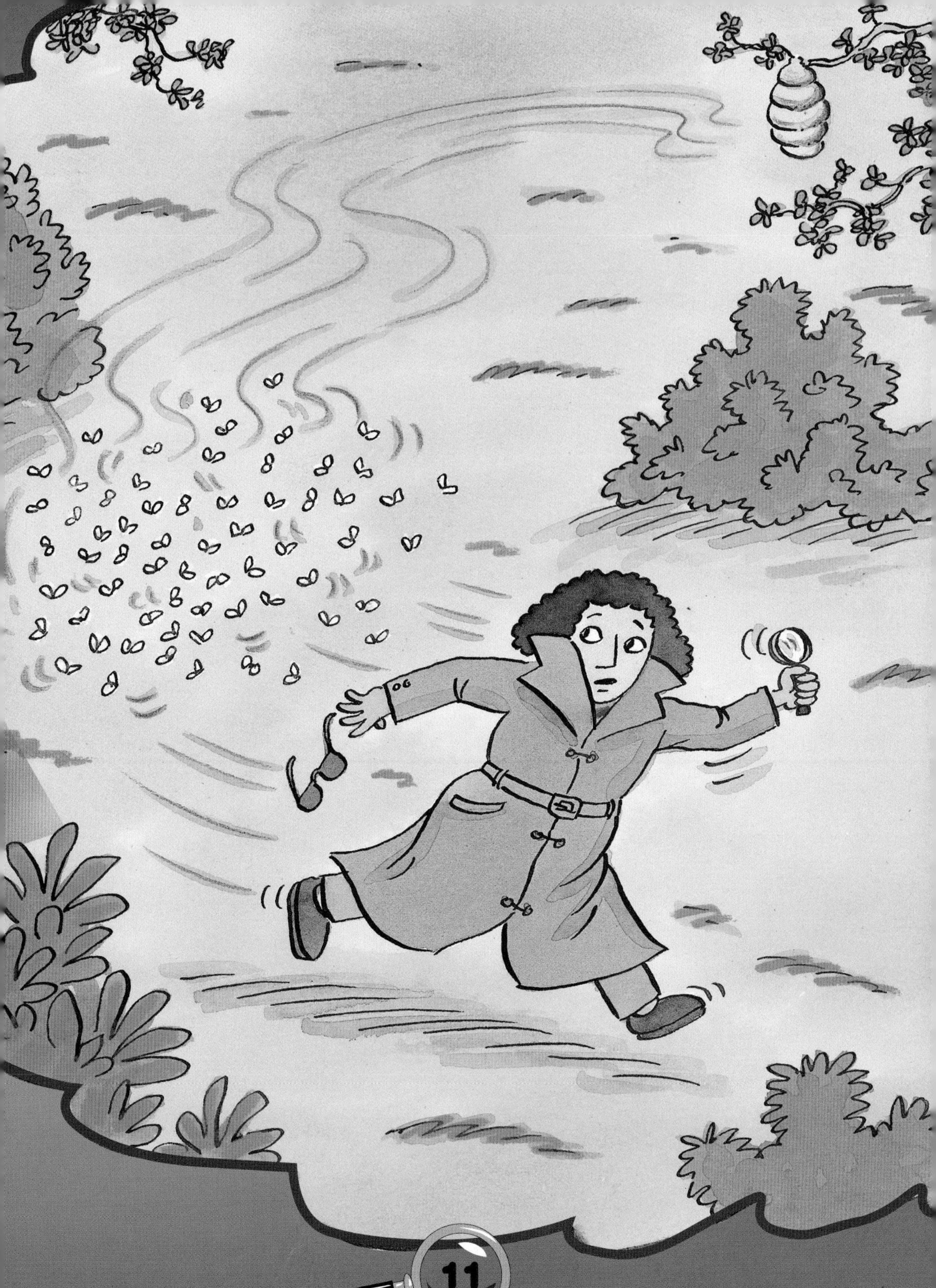

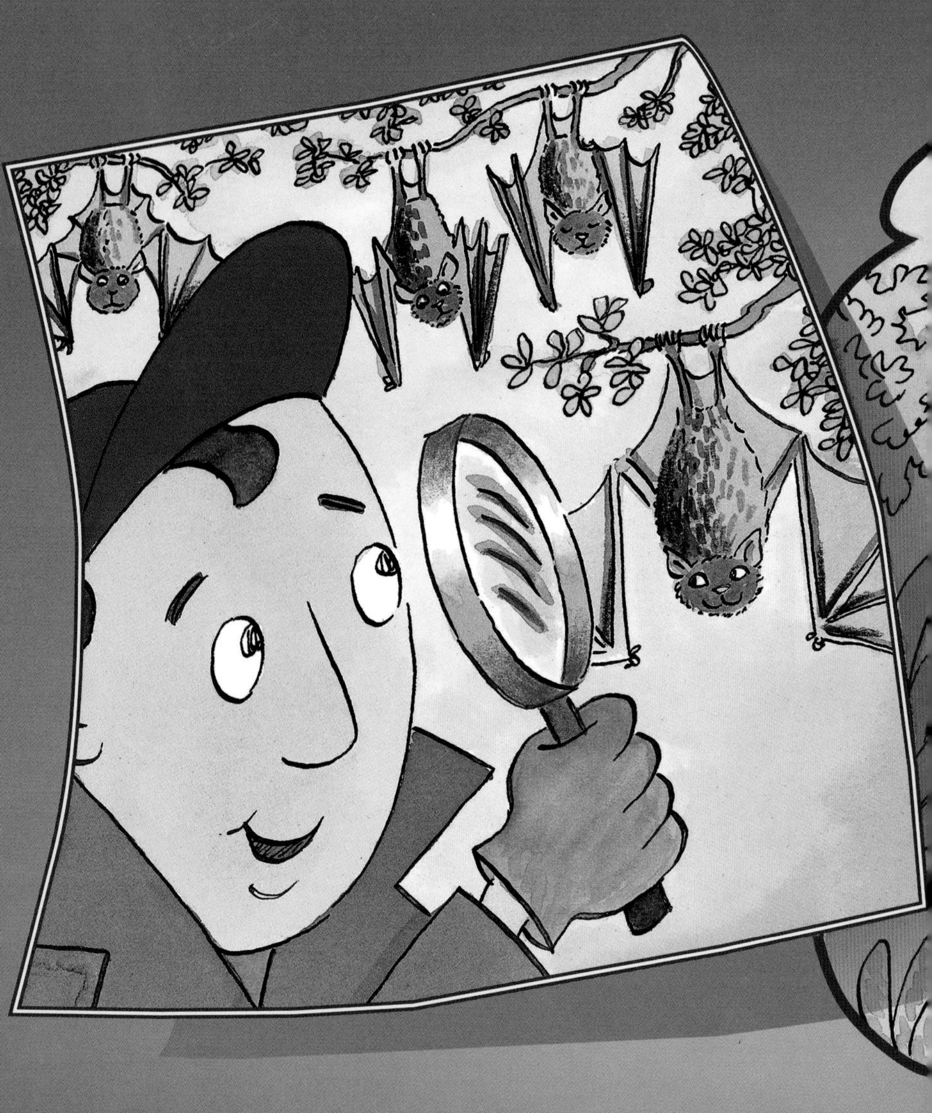

Here are the bats.

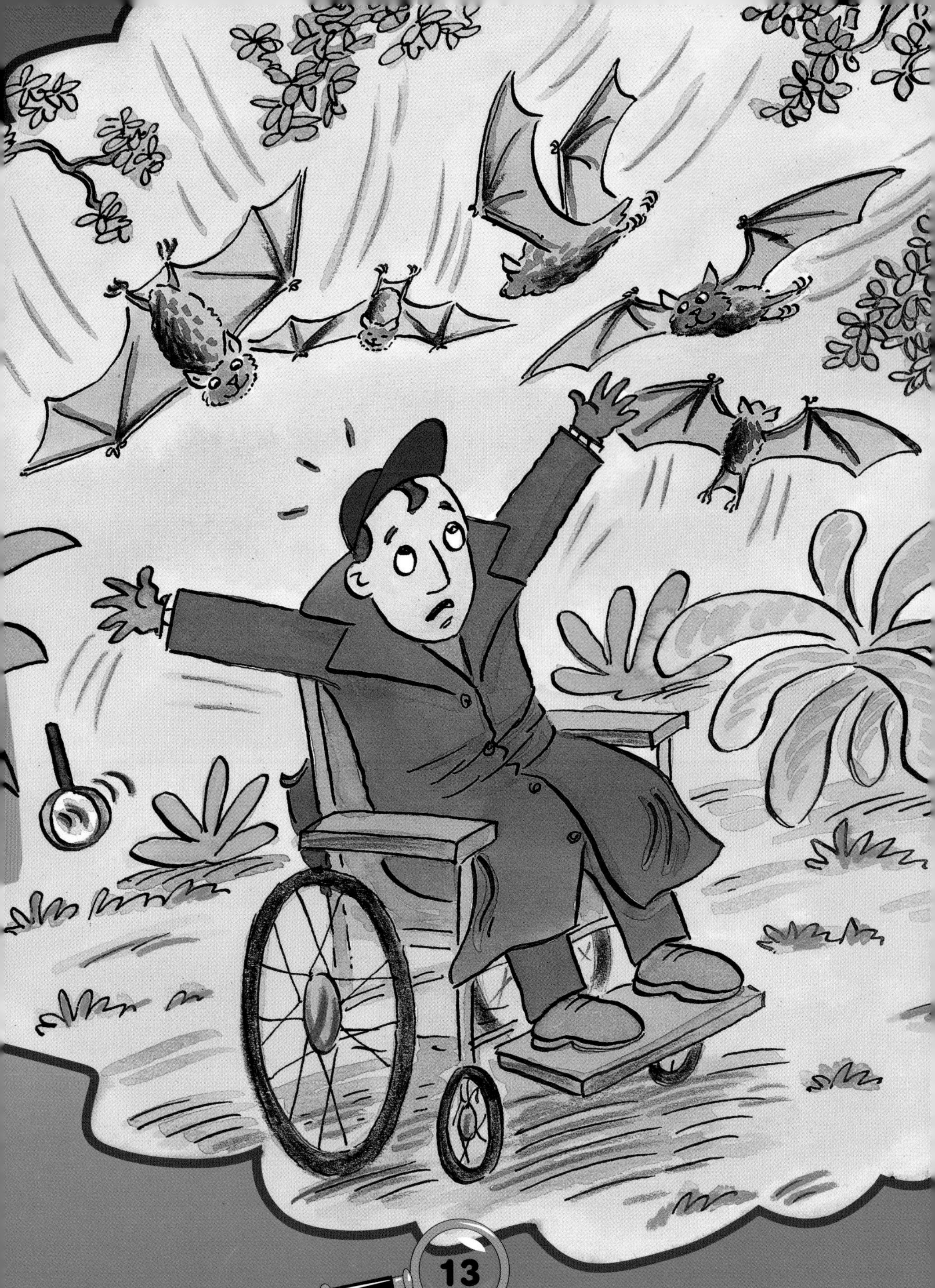

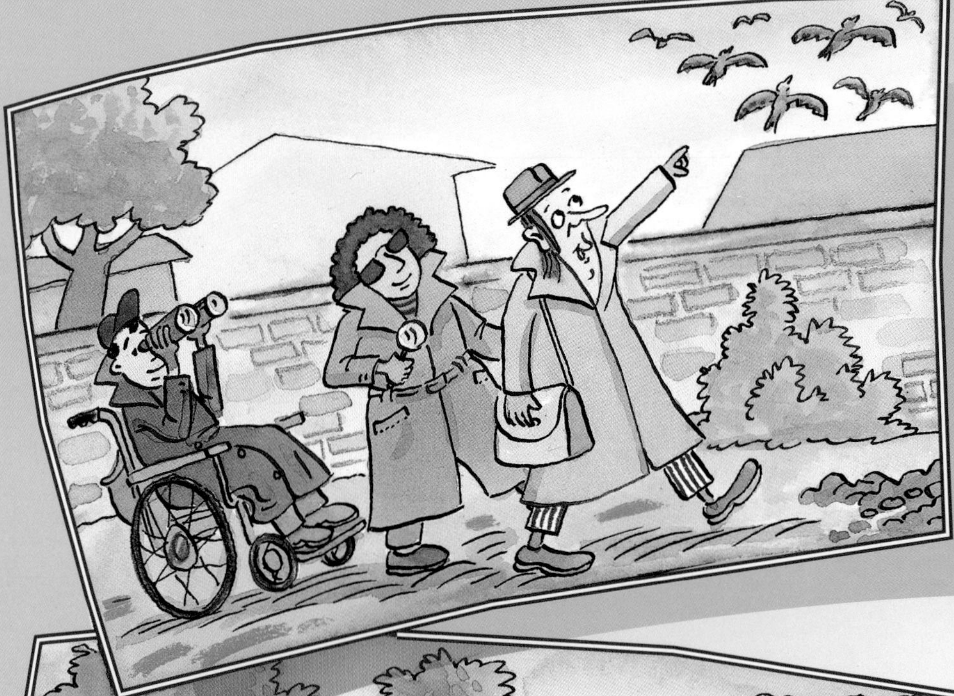

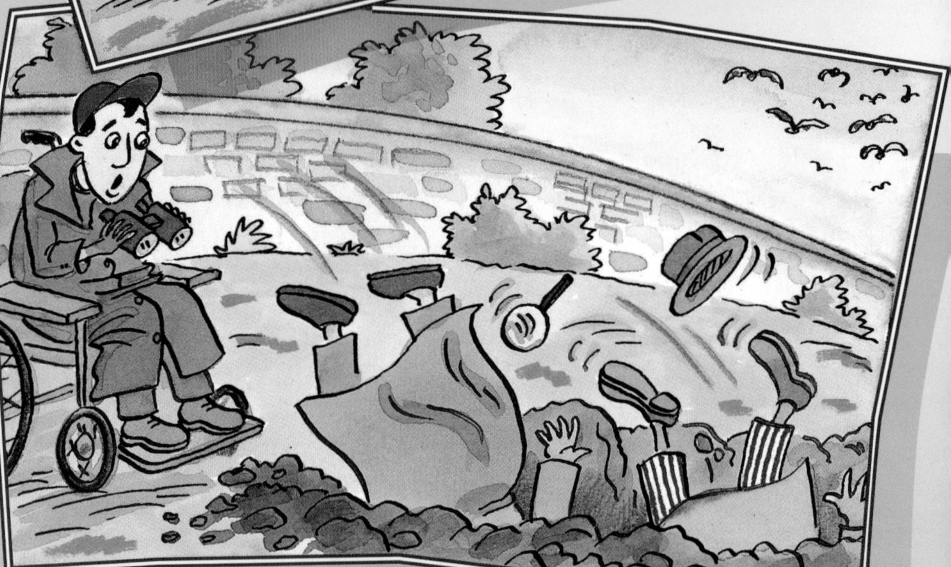

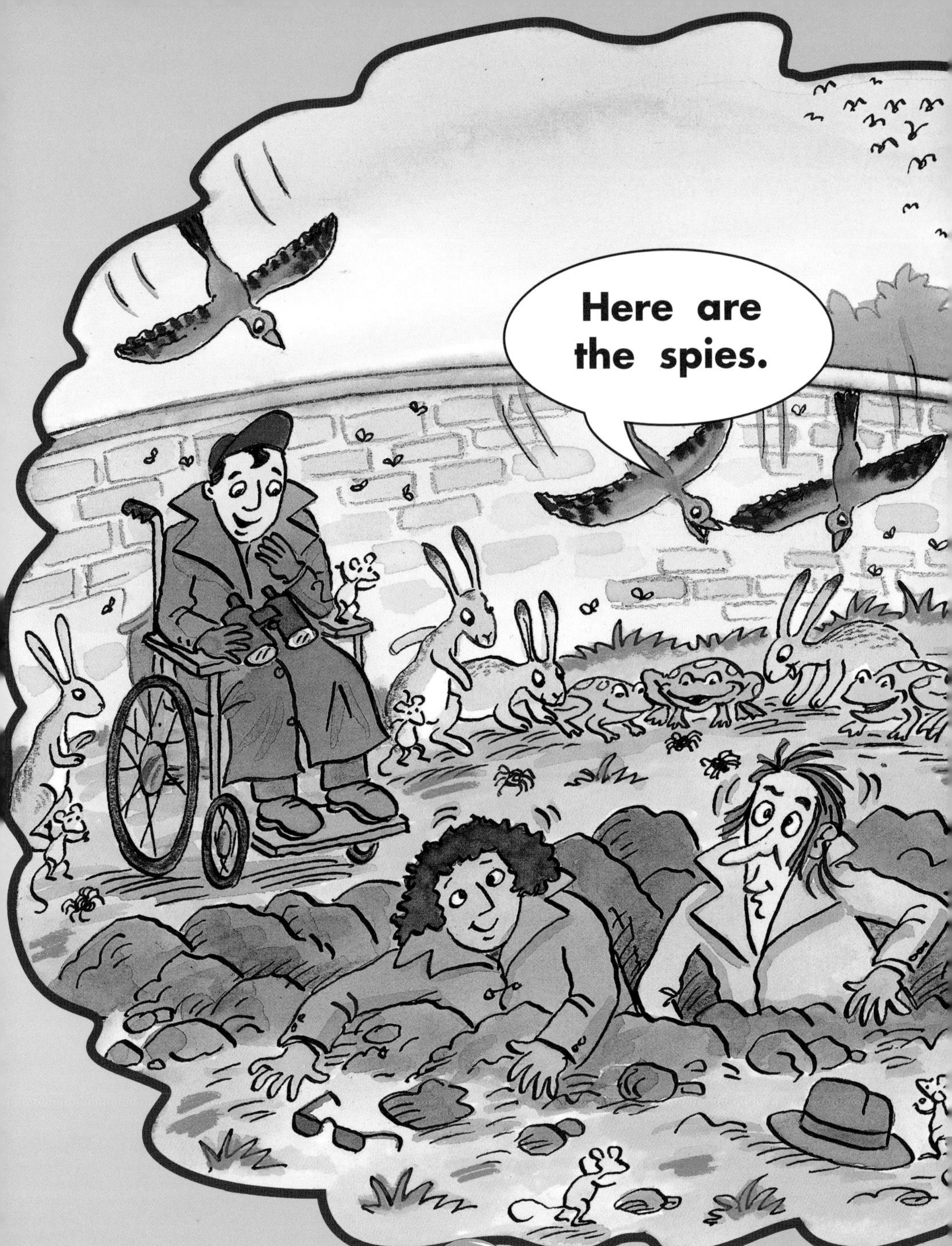
Here are the spies.

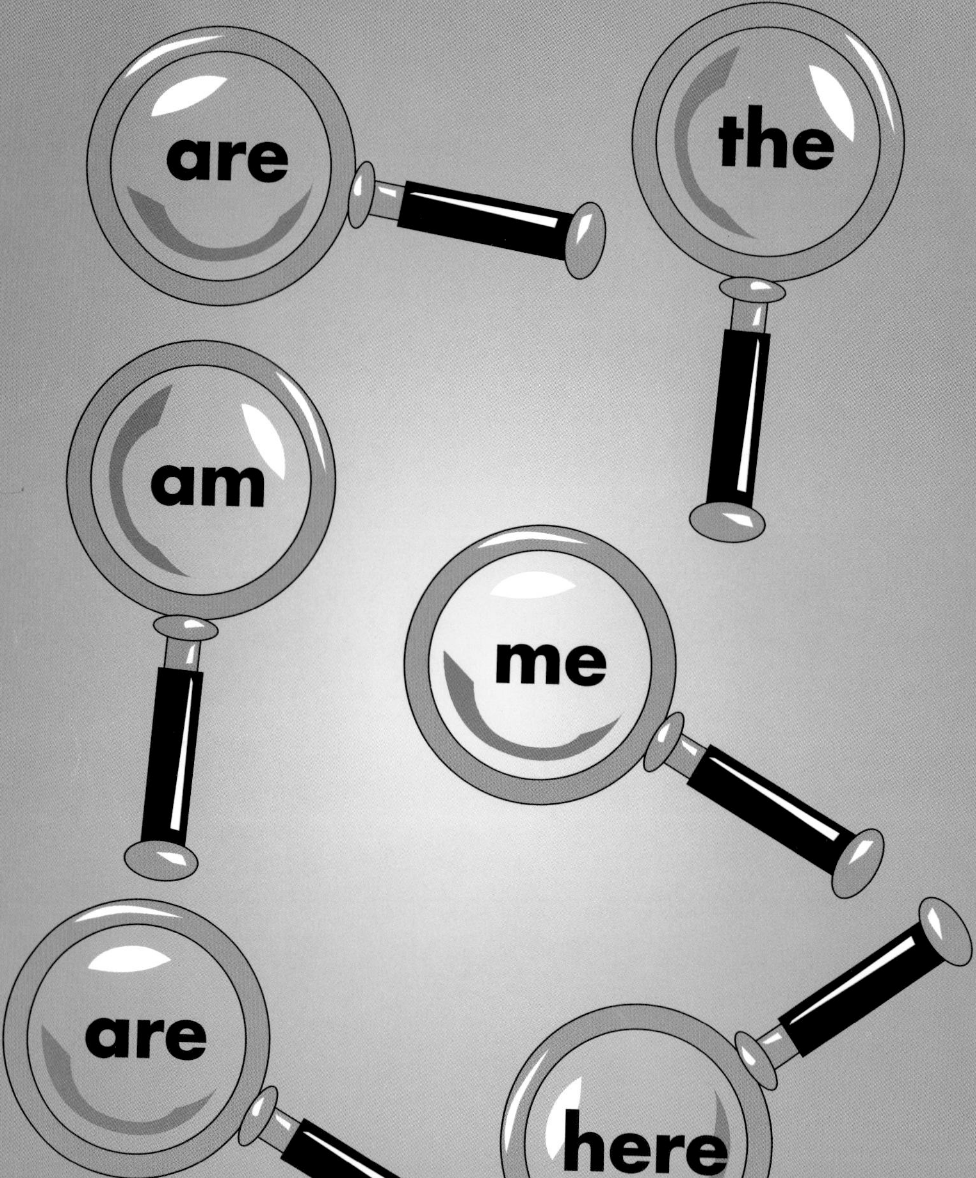
are
the
am
me
are
here